SCOOBY-DOO!™

and the

CUPCAKE CAPER

DEVELOPING READER
LEVEL 2
250-750 WORDS

D0191304

By Sonia Sander
Illustrated by Duendes del Sur

WORLDWIDE PUBLISHING
WB

SCHOLASTIC INC.
New York Toronto London Auckland
Sydney Mexico City New Delhi Hong Kong

ISBN 978-0-545-22523-6

Designed by Michael Massen

12 11 10 9 8 7 6 5 4 3 2 1   10 11 12 13 14 15/0

Printed in U.S.A.   40
First printing, July 2010

"Come on, gang," called Fred. "The school's Halloween cupcake bake-off is about to begin."

"Like, I hope we didn't forget anything," said Shaggy.

"Don't worry, Shaggy," said Daphne. "The school has a fully-stocked cooking pantry."

"This should be just the right amount of batter for cupcakes," said the school cook, Gloria Grill. "If you need more, come find me. I'm the only one with a key to the pantry."

"Like, these are the flattest cupcakes ever," said Shaggy.

"I wonder what went wrong," said Daphne.

"Jinkies, look at this box!" cried Velma. "We used salt, not baking soda!"

"Sorry, kids," said Fred. "I guess we have to start again."

W-h-i-i-i-r-r-r! W-h-i-i-i-r-r-r!
Just as the gang got back to work, all the mixers came on.
Batter flew all over the room.
"Ruh-roh!" barked Scooby.
"Like, take cover!" cried Shaggy.

"It's the ghost! It's the ghost!" the students shouted.

"Zoinks!" said Shaggy. "No one told us there was a ghost."

"A creepy ghost has been hanging around ever since the bake sale was announced," a boy in a monster costume explained.

"Well, bake sale or no bake sale, we're out of here! Right, Scoob?" cried Shaggy.

"Hang on, gang! First things first," said Fred. "Let's stop these crazy mixers."

Fred tried to unplug the mixers. But they were all on a timer.

"Looks like someone set the mixers to go off," said Velma.

"Someone or *something*?" said Shaggy.

"Maybe Shaggy is right," said Daphne. "We've just been warned. COOK AT YOUR OWN RISK!"

"It looks like we have a mystery to solve," said Fred.

"Like, I was afraid he was going to say that," said Shaggy.

"Let's split up," said Fred. "Shaggy and Scooby, try the pantry."

Shaggy was glad to get out of the kitchen. But not after he and Scooby came face to face with the ghost!

"Like, run, Scoob!" cried Shaggy. "It's that spooky ghost!"

Soon the ghost was chasing the whole gang.

"Quick, into the lab!" called Fred. "Look for a place to hide!"

Scooby and the gang hid in a closet.
The ghost ran right by their hiding spot.

"Is it me, or is that ghost falling apart?"
asked Daphne.

All Scooby and Shaggy knew was they
smelled food.

"Like, that ghost leaves one yummy trail," said Shaggy.

"Ruh-huh," slurped Scooby.

As she watched Scooby and Shaggy clean up after the ghost, Velma had an idea.

"I have just the thing to catch our ghost," said Velma.

"Like, do you really think a big, creepy ghost is going to be afraid of teeny, tiny ants?" asked Shaggy.

"Trust me," said Velma, "a lot of little ants make one strong army."

The ants did their job.
Soon the ghost was too itchy to get away.
Scooby and Shaggy dragged in a fire hose.
They gave the ghost a good wash.

The ghost was cleaned off in no time. "I had a feeling Gloria Grill was behind this," said Velma. "The key to the case was her key to the empty pantry."

"I was sure my cupcakes would win the bake sale, but only kids were allowed to enter!" said Gloria Grill. "My plan to ruin the sale would've worked if it weren't for you meddling kids!"

With the mystery solved, the gang got back to work.

Soon the kitchen was full of cupcakes.

"Jeepers," said Daphne, "it would be so hard to pick the best cupcake."

"You're right, Daphne," said Shaggy. "Like, I think we need to try each flavor one more time. You really need two tastes to pick the best one."

"Ruh-huh," agreed Scooby. "Scooby-Dooby-Doo!"